PIRATES IN CLASSROOM 3

For Yvonne, Jenny, David and Tom, B.W

For Kenzie, Gemma and Alex, with love A.D

Written by Alison ~~WITHDRAWN~~ ed by Ben Whitehouse

Classroom 3 erupted with noise when
Ms. Bitsy left the room.

Alex and his classmates laughed and chased and played.

THUD.

"What was that?" cried Hugo.

"Someone's at the window," said Alex.

"Pssssst, open up!"

The children gasped. It was a...

...pirate!

"Ahoy mateys! I'm Captain Calamity

and I'm searching for treasure!"

"Isn't treasure buried at the bottom of the ocean?" asked Cai.

"Or on a desert island?" asked Zoe.

"Well, yes," said the captain, "But the man who gave me this map clearly said:"

"You will find buried treasure,
In classroom 3.
Under the sea
Is where the treasure will be."

GOLD GUINEAS ONLY!!!

"What sea?" asked Alex.

"We don't even have a swimming pool," said Lucy.

"Oh no!" cried Captain Calamity,

"I'll never find it before Pirate Bloodloss!"

"Who's Pirate Bloodloss?" asked Alex.

Captain Calamity quivered.

"A **REALLY** mean and scary pirate."

"We'll help you!" cried the children.

They all gathered around the map.

"You're in the right place," said Alex, "Here's our school."

"Phew," sighed Captain Calamity.

They **rummaged** through the reading corner.

They **sifted** and
strained the sand.

They **burrowed** through the building blocks.

"We'll never find it,"

whimpered Captain Calamity.

Alex stopped and studied the alphabet.

A, B, C, D... his eyes rested again on the letter C.

"C," he said. "It's under the C! Look everyone!

Under the C is where the treasure will be!"

Alex tugged and heaved until the letter C
came off and revealed a lever.
Alex pulled the lever and...

Pop! The floorboards opened.

"The sea!" cried Captain Calamity.

"Quick, let's go before Ms. Bitsy gets back," cried the children.

"Ms. Bitsy **IS** back," said Ms. Bitsy.

"And if you're searching for treasure..."

...then *I'm* coming *too*!" The children cheered!

"Ladies first," Captain Calamity blushed.

They **slipped** and **slid**.

They **plunged**
down,
down,
down
into a **deep**
blue sea.

They **ducked**, they **dodged** and they **dove.**

Until...

They found the **treasure**!

"One, two, three, HEAVE," cried Captain Calamity.

They pushed the treasure all the way back to the classroom.

"Great work me mateys!" said Captain Calamity.

But the classroom was not empty.

"**Arrrr**, I see you've brought me my treasure,"
said a rather mean and scary looking pirate.

"Ahh! It's Bloodloss!" cried Captain Calamity.
But Class 3 were not scared. They knew
someone who could handle any pirate bully!

Ms. Bitsy!

"There is **no bullying** in my classroom. Off you go Bloodloss or I will tell your parents!"

"Argh! Not Mummy," cried Bloodloss.

He scampered off and all the children cheered.

"Captain," Alex said.
"I think there's more treasure!"

"But why, lad?"
asked Captain Calamity.

"Because X *always* marks the spot!" said Alex.

Pirates in Classroom 3
An original concept by author Alison Donald
© Alison Donald
Illustrated by Ben Whitehouse

MAVERICK ARTS PUBLISHING LTD
Studio 3A, City Business Centre, 6 Brighton Road, Horsham, West Sussex, RH13 5BB
© Maverick Arts Publishing Limited   +44 (0)1403 256941

Published October 2017

A CIP catalogue record for this book is available at the British Library.

ISBN 978-1-84886-247-0

Oh Ms. Bitsy...
You were so brave!

Call me Daphne.

Maverick
arts publishing
www.maverickbooks.co.uk

OWL

The Human Brain
and Spinal Cord